TRACY M. JOYCE

PIO

TALES OF ALTAICA

A COMPANION SERIES TO
THE CHRONICLES OF ALTAICA

Published by Cassilis and Co in 2023

A Cataloguing-in-Publication entry is available from the National Library of Australia

ISBN: 978-0-9924619-9-7 (pbk) ISBN: 978-0-9924619-8-0 (ebook)

Cover design by Karri Klawiter (www.artbykarri.com)

Map of Altaica by Misty Beee

For Robert

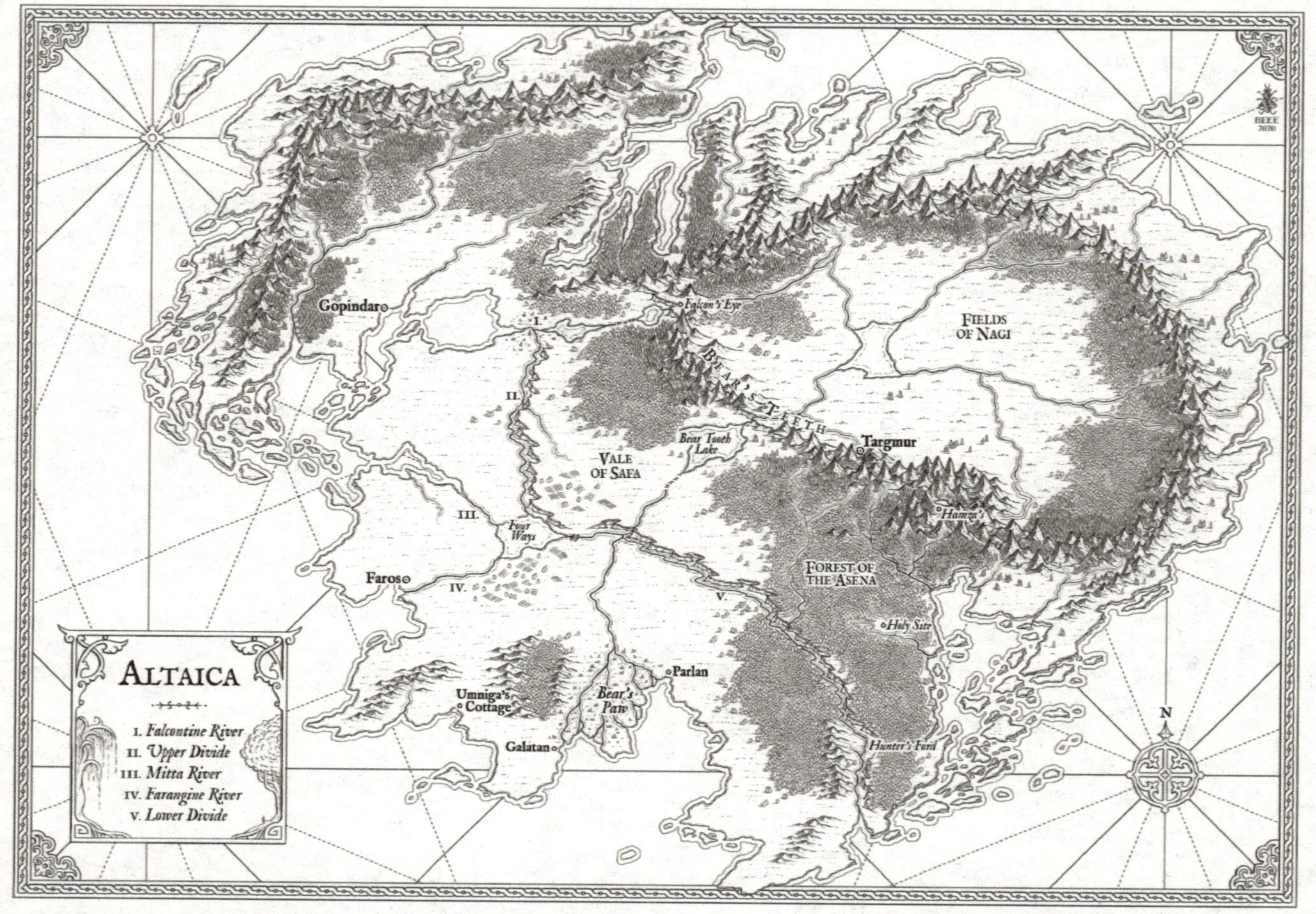
Gopindar
Falcon's Eye
FIELDS OF NAGI
BEAR'S TEETH
Bear Tooth Lake
VALE OF SAFA
Targmur
Hamza's
Four Ways
FOREST OF THE ASENA
Faros
Holy Site
Parlan
Umniga's Cottage
Bear's Paw
Galatan
Hunter's Ford
N
ALTAICA
i. Falcontine River
ii. Upper Divide
iii. Mitta River
iv. Farangine River
v. Lower Divide

CONTENTS

PREAMBLE

YOU'LL NEED TO READ this bit...

For those of you who haven't read *Altaica* and *Asena Blessed*, you need to know that at this point, the clans of Altaica are at war. Most children are being evacuated from the war zone by Hamza, a muleteer.

However Pio, a refugee boy with untapped magical abilities, and his best friend Kiriz, avoided the evacuation with dire consequences.

Having been rescued from kidnappers, Pio—along with his mother and Kiriz—are now being escorted the safety of Hamza's home. Their escorts are Asena – legendary wolf-like creatures. They are traversing the slopes of The Bear's Teeth Mountain Range in order to avoid trouble.

CHAPTER ONE

IN THE CHILL AIR of the autumn morning, Pio, Kiriz and Lucia rode their horses, with the Matriarch of the pack leading the way and several Asena flanking them. A group of Asena scouted the way forward, while overhead, Fiamma, Pio's guardian, swooped and dived through the air, her high pitch cries of joy carrying to those below. Pio felt the falcon prod his mind before his head swam with her vision, and he looked down upon himself through her eyes. She stared ahead, revealing the vast mountains and forest awaiting them which were backed by endless blue sky. Fiamma's vision filed down to a young shrew on the mountainside. Pio's stomach lurched.

Let me go, Fiamma. If you're going to eat, then let me go.

Puzzlement filtered down to him through their link, along with the notion that hunting was fun, but she released him.

Pio turned in the saddle to check on Lucia. Days of riding had left his mother rumpled and hollow-eyed; she moved as though she was ancient.

"Pio, did you ride in your old home?" Kiriz asked.

"In Penīdīen? Not really. Not unless a quiet farm horse had come to Pa's forge for shoeing. Then I'd sometimes have a bit of a trot around. But I was never allowed out of sight of Pa or to go fast," he said with an eye roll.

"Why not?"

"Not our horses, see. And Pa didn't want them—" he put on a gruff voice, "looking like they'd run a dozen races and were about to drop."

Kiriz crowed with delight. "You got caught!"

"Yes, he did, Kiriz," said Lucia, "and he could barely sit for a week."

Pio sighed. "And I had to clean out the farmer's pigsties for a week."

"Pio, don't fib," Lucia said. "It was only a couple of days. Thank the gods because he stank!"

"I got to ride the farm horse we had, but I could never get her to go fast," Kiriz said.

The vast Forest of the Asena surrounded them, and this section was predominantly pine trees, so there was almost no undergrowth. They followed a deer trail that meandered along the side of the steep slope before angling down. The pines gradually thinned, and deciduous saplings with a few autumn leaves struggled to reach the slim light. The horses picked their way quietly down the slope. Lucia squealed as her mount skidded on the bed of pine needles.

Pio laughed as his horse did the same. "It's like ice skating!"

"Don't worry, Lucia," Kiriz called. "Your horse will just follow Pio's."

The Matriarch guided them through boulders bigger than men, and over a broad silver-streaked vein of white rock that winked in the sunshine. Their path dropped sharply down a ridgeline.

"No, no, no," Lucia whispered, but Pio heard her gasp. "Oh! I'm going to fall off. I can feel myself tipping over!"

When Pio looked back, his mother's eyes were closed in terror. "Put your feet forward, Ma! Remember the lessons. Feet forward going down, lean back a bit. The horse has... um... plenty of self-preservation, so we'll be fine. Besides, the Matriarch wouldn't bring us down here unless it was safe."

Lucia, face twisted in fear, gripped the saddle in one hand and leaned back so far Pio thought she was almost lying down. "I never thought I'd be putting my safety in the hands of a wolf," Lucia muttered.

"Remember, they're not wolves," Pio said. "Ma, they're our friends. You've got to stop worrying about them. They'll get us to Hamza's safe and sound. Wait and see."

"You sound just like your father."

"Open your eyes, Ma! It's not far, then we turn sideways and it's easier."

Lucia opened one eye. Dislodged rocks careened down the ridgeline.

"Oh, gods! We'll be killed, I know it!" Lucia said.

"Ma, you're green as grass," Pio said as his horse turned right and disappeared off the trail.

Lucia squeaked in terror.

"Just keep your feet forward," Kiriz said. "Or maybe look at the view, not the ground."

"Look at the view?" Dismay spiked Lucia's words.

"Yes! It's wonderful. I was scared of the hill, but when I looked ahead it's not so bad," the little girl said.

"It's not a hill, it's a mountain! And we're almost on top!"

"No, were not. There's heaps of hill above us."

"And even more below! Oh! Why did they bring us so high up?" Lucia said.

"Just sit up a bit and keep your feet forward," Kiriz said. "I promise it will be better."

Lucia raised her head and took in the horizon, drawing a harsh intake of breath. "Oh my!" she said. Her gaze strayed downward.

Lucia swayed in the saddle, hunching over.

"Lucia! Don't look down, just straight ahead. Pio stop!" Kiriz yelled. "Lucia, you can do this! You passed the combat trials and made it into the Bear Clan. Not everyone can do that. You're brave! Just look ahead. You can do it!"

Lucia's hands gripped the pommel of the saddle, but she straightened. "I did, didn't I."

"Take a big breath in and out. That's what my ma used to say. Or think of a song and sing it."

"Sing?"

"Or hum." Kiriz began singing a simple melody and Lucia slowly hummed along trying to catch the words and meaning. "That's it!" Kiriz laughed. "Although you just said crow when it's really cow."

Annoyance flicked across Lucia's face. "Kiriz, I'm still learning. It's really not nice to —"

They rounded the corner and caught up with a grinning Pio, waiting on a level section of track.

"Ma, how does a crow get milked?"

"Oh, stop it the pair of you!" Lucia said.

"But you made it, Lucia!" Kiriz said. "If you can go down that bit the rest will be easy."

Lucia looked back up the mountainside, hands still clinging to the saddle and a small, relieved, smile creased her lips. "Maybe you're right, but I think I'll need both your cheekiness and games to get me through next time."

The Bear's Teeth Mountains towered to their left; the peaks surrounded in cloud. On the next ridge over, spindly spruce clung tenaciously to the rocky slopes here and there. Wildflowers jutted from cracks in the rocks

where soil had built up and golden lichen covered boulders. Mountain goats balanced on the precipitous slopes
while they grazed. Amazed, Lucia and Kiriz gaped as
one leaped down the mountainside, landed on a boulder,
then jumped and raced along the slope, sending scree
flying.

"Look on the left. See the eagles!" Kiriz said.

Fiamma screeched and pulled from her dive to land on
Pio's shoulder; her feathers ruffled and her eyes tracked
the eagles.

Below them soared a pair of wedge-tailed eagles, their
massive wings extended as they circled lazily. One dived,
aiming for a kid on the slopes who'd strayed too far from
its mother. As the bird homed in on the young goat,
talons extended, the doe looked up and charged, bat-
tering the predator. The eagle gouged and pecked at the
goat as they tumbled about. Meanwhile, the second bird
snatched the kid in its talons and flew off, screeching.
The first eagle and the doe broke apart as they tumbled
down the hill and the bird gained the sky to join its mate.

"Did it get away?" Kiriz said plaintively.

"I can hear it, Kiriz," Lucia said. "The mother goat
survived. She is calling for her baby."

Kiriz said nothing, merely hung her head.

→

Ishir, a lean recruit, barely sixteen, with wispy stubble,
looked over his shoulder, stopped, and peered about the
trees. "I hate this place. Dhanuk, how far in this damn
forest do you want to go?"

"Far enough that no one finds us." Dhanuk halted, looking back at Ishir and Parv. "We're deserters, so we'll give it a while, then do some scouting and see if the war's over and sneak back home. I'm not dying for Ratilal. He's done nothing for me," Dhanuk said.

Parv clapped a hand on Ishir's shoulder. "Come on, boy. We'll find a good campsite farther up the mountain so we've got a vantage point, and sit the war out."

"The deeper we go in this bloody forest the edgier I feel," Ishir said. "This is the Forest of the Asena. What in the name of all the gods are we going to do if we meet one?"

Dhanuk shook his head. "Oh, come off it! No one's seen an Asena in these parts for centuries."

"Yeah, stop being such a whiney sod, Ishir," Parv said. "We're scouts and we're scouting. If anyone finds us that's what we'll say."

They hiked deeper into the forest. The scent of pine enveloped them and the pine needles muted their steps.

Ishir's foot sunk into a patch of mud. "What the—"

Parv laughed. "It's just a spring, boy. You can see it seeping up from between those boulders."

The older warrior led him to the rocks. A spring burbled out of the ground, it's rivulet running along a groove in the soil and then veering downhill. "Listen. You can hear a creek down there."

The boy canted his head, nodding, taking stock of his surrounding, inhaling deeply. "I can smell the damp from here too."

"Good! Think about those things. Catalogue what you see as we walk and stop thinking about Asena. I'll turn you into a proper scout into by the time we leave here."

Dhanuk scowled. "He is a proper scout, Parv. He's passed the training."

Parv scoffed. "On his own? I don't think so. You babied him along and did him no favours."

Finger pointed a Parv, Dhanuk said, "Just remember, we were *all* like him once."

Parv's lip curled, before he turned a smile on Ishir. "It's like Dhanuk said. The Asena have not been here for years and they've no reason to come back."

Ishir slumped. "You're right."

They moved off. Something thick and damp, hit Ishir's forehead. "Great! I've just been shat on by bird!" He wiped his brow and his hand came away bloody. The colour drained from his face. "It's blood!"

Another wet lump hit him and he flicked a red, blob of meaty fat from his head. Ishir jumped slideways and slipped in the spring.

Parv laughed, but Dhanuk ran to Ishir and hauled the shaking young man to his feet.

Dhanuk pointed to the top of the nearest pine. "Look, there's an eagle's nest up there. I'd say they just dropped a bit of their dinner on you."

Ishir hung his head. "You must think I'm still wet behind the ears, too."

Dhanuk wrapped an arm around him. "No. You've spooked yourself remembering old wives' tales about the Asena and then had gore dropped on you. I reckon that'd give most a fright." His glanced at Parv. "Though they'd not admit it."

"We should stop here and set up a camp back there under that pine," Parv said. "Lots of nice sturdy branches to make a quick shelter, and I've seen plenty of animal trails."

"Good idea." Dhanuk said.

The three of them set up camp, tossing a canvas ground sheet over a branch and pegging it out. They cut pine branches and leaned them against the sturdy limb, creating a tent of green over the canvas and layering the branches along one end. Ishir dug a fire pit while Parv gathered dry, fallen wood.

"I'm off looking for dinner," Dhanuk said.

"Dodging work?" Parv asked.

"Hunting," Dhanuk said, a hard glint in his eye. "I'll check what other game is about."

"Sure. We'll work on the campsite while you're off wandering," Parv said.

"Cut it out," Dhanuk said. "You know I'll do my share and give you a hand when I get back. I'll see if I can't get a rabbit or two." Dhanuk disappeared into the woods.

Ishir, unbundled his bed roll.

"You should be grateful, lad," Parv said, laying a hand on Ishir's shoulder. "Dhanuk promised your sister he'd keep you safe and he is."

"I know," Ishir said. He sat back on his heels and looked at the curly haired giant. "But I wanted to fight. Everyone thinks I'm useless and need looking after. If I fought and returned home, better still, came home a hero, then they'd lay off me. And maybe I'd actually impress a girl instead of them laughing and going off with some tough-looking, handsome bloke."

Parv sighed. "One: you are not useless, or you wouldn't have got into the scouts—"

"But you said—"

"Two: heroes usually don't come home. Three: well... I haven't got a three, but be patient."

CHAPTER TWO

"Go and fill the water bottles. Don't wander off. Stick together," Lucia said as she hunted for fallen wood for their night fire.

"Yes, Ma!" Pio said.

"We've got an Asena to guard us, what does she reckon is going to happen?" Kiriz muttered. "Where do you think the other Asena went?"

"I dunno. Hunting maybe."

They wandered down to the creek.

"Here's a good spot," Pio said. "It's deep enough to fill the flasks."

Kiriz grinned and shook her head. "No. Let's find a better one where there's a bit more current and the water is clearer."

Pio frowned and stared at the small pool before them. "It looks fine."

"No. I'm sure it doesn't."

The frown fell from Pio's face and he laughed. "Next time just say you want to go exploring."

"No, because we can use that line about the water to convince your ma about why we took so long." Kiriz giggled and ran along the creek. "Come on!"

They came upon a larger pool, further down the slope.

"We should stop here. I think we're too far from camp."

Kiriz put her hands on her hips. "It's not that far."

Pio knelt, filled the flasks, then sat and dangled his feet in the cool water. Kiriz stood, arms crossed, tapping her foot.

"You can do that all you want, but I'm not moving," Pio said.

Kiriz rolled her eyes and sat beside him. "Fine!"

Fiamma fluttered down and landed on Pio's outstretched arm. She canted her head, staring at him. Pio grew still and closed his eyes. He nodded and the bird took flight.

"What was that?" Kiriz asked.

"She wants to hunt before dark."

"She asked your permission? Does she have to?"

"Of course not! Fiamma is free, but she wanted me to join with her while she hunts."

"Join with her?" Kiriz took off her boots and put her feet in the water.

"We kind of connect our minds and I can see what she sees, but we did it once before when she hunted and I could feel her chewing and eating a raw rabbit guts and all." Kiriz grimaced. "I got queasy. So, I'm happy for her to hunt on her own. She'll come back when she's done."

Pio took out his flute and played a song that idled along the river — tranquil, soothing, yet alive. The forest quietened at their intrusion, but as the music waltzed through the trees, the birds chirped more loudly and small finches alighted on branches near them, their dark, bright eyes taking in Pio. Kiriz held her breath as one landed on her knee. A fox poked its head out of a fern patch. Their Asena guard spun in a circle and lay on soft moss, under the shelter of a bush, hidden from view.

Kiriz squealed. The wild animals bolted.

"Kiriz!" Pio said.

"Sorry, something nibbled on my foot in the water."

Pio looked down. "I didn't feel anything and I can't see anything!"

"There was! I swear!" She pulled her foot from the water. "Play your song. I'll try to see if something's in there."

"Everything will have run away. They probably heard your scream for miles."

She punched him. "Just play!"

"All right! Don't hit me again, that hurt!"

Pio played, and the birdsong returned, though the finches stayed well away from Kiriz.

Out of the reeds of the river swam a large trout. It came straight to Pio and lazily hovered in the water before him. When he stopped playing, it darted away. "I've got an idea. Get in the water."

"What! Why?"

"Do you want rabbit again for dinner? Or fish?"

"Oh! You think I can catch it?"

"If you're quick. Stand just in there," he said. "I'll see if I can get it to come back."

Kiriz waded into the pool, stood legs apart with her hands poised to snatch dinner from the water.

Eying the pond, Pio played the same tune, willing the fish to reappear. The trilling of finches increased as more birds landed on branches near the creek.

Water rippled near Kiriz's leg. She bent closer to its surface, searching. "Oh, there you are," she whispered. "It's working, but he's moving too much to grab. Maybe you can put him to sleep."

Pio stopped playing. "Are you saying my music is boring?"

"No, but it's clearly magic. So, make him sleep."

Pio's stomach lurched at the word *magic* and his music stuttered. Everyone from home hated magic. The old sorcerers had laid waste to vast sections of the countryside in the ancient battles. *Magic. Evil.* But he wasn't evil and how could music hurt? Isa wasn't evil. She saved people with her skills, but not even Ma and Pa were happy when they first found out. *What will people say?*

He lowered his flute and looked at Kiriz. "I never thought it was magic," he whispered.

She straightened and stared at him. "So? What's the big deal? The Wild is everywhere around us, and here it's special to be able to use it."

Pio swallowed nervously. "It's just that at home it's a bad thing. Evil. No one has it anymore or doesn't say so if they do, and anyone thought to have magic is shunned... or worse."

"Worse?"

"They die."

"You mean they're killed?"

Pio nodded.

"Look, that's not your home anymore. *This* is your home. Here, being able to use the Wild in any way is the best thing ever! Do you think Umniga was evil? Asha? And Isa, what about her?"

"No, none of them is evil."

"Well, there you are then! What are you waiting for? You're meant to be the next bard kenati and you've got to start practising some time. Besides, I really don't want rabbit again for dinner." She waded to him, grabbed the flute and held it to his lips. "Now play. Please."

"All right."

"Great! Fish it is!" Grinning, Kiriz moved into position, poised over the water.

Pio's melody blossomed and beckoned.

"He's back," she whispered.

The tune lulled and formed a soft, circular pattern. It spoke of safety, rest, contentment. Pio felt a faint, pulsing vibration in his pocket from the flame eye crystal fragments he'd carried since Isaura's guardian, Alejo, had broken the original crystal. They thrummed in time with his music. He resisted the urge to take them out and examine them as Isa's words rang in his mind. *Don't play with them and don't show them to anyone, not even Kiriz.*

He continued his tune, content with the knowledge he wasn't playing with them. *I can't help it if they do this. I'm not breaking her rules.*

Kiriz's shoulders slumped and she swayed in the water.

Pio's eyes glinted mischievously. He kept playing. The Asena, in deep sleep, snored. Kiriz drooped, her legs folded, and she fell into the pool.

With a splash, she regained her senses, soaking wet and spluttering water.

"Not me! We want the fish asleep, or something... still," Kiriz said.

"Sorry," Pio said, smirking.

"You did that on purpose!"

"No! I just don't know what I'm doing. I'm still figuring things out."

Pio recommenced playing and focused his thoughts on the fish. It swam back toward him and as it neared Kiriz, Pio recaptured the soft, lullaby holding-pattern. Kiriz rubbed her eyes and yawned but remained standing. The Asena beside him rolled over half asleep.

It's better, but they're still affected.

Kiriz grinned as the fish halted in front of her. Her hands flashed downward and she snatched it from the water. It wriggled in her grasp. She wobbled and fell backwards into the pool, flinging the fish toward the bank. It flew and slapped Pio in the face.

Kiriz waded out. "That fish better taste good."

"It's not rabbit, so it will taste good," Pio said, shoving a stick through its gills to carry it.

Lucia ran down to the creek, pushing her way through waist-high ferns. "What's wrong? Are you hurt?"

Pio and Kiriz stared at her pale, frightened face.

"Um, no," Pio said.

Lucia glared at them. "Not hurt, in any way? Then why did one of you make that unholy screech?"

Kiriz gulped. "I fell in the creek."

Pio rolled his eyes. "You didn't squeal about that! You just got frightened by a fish!"

Kiriz shoved Pio. "If you'd been in the creek, you would've yelped too!"

"Enough! And why are you all the way down here? It took ages to find you! Get back to the campsite, both of you. I'm not letting you leave it again today. Kiriz, we need to get you dry." They hung their heads. "Move it. Now!" Lucia crossed her arms and tapped her foot. "You've got until I count to three."

"Come on, Kiriz. You don't want her to get to three. You won't be able to sit for a week."

The two raced back to camp.

Lucia sighed, looking at the dozing Asena. "Well, you're supposed to be looking after them. Couldn't you do something?"

It peeled one eye open to look at her, rose sedately, stretched, and nudged her back to camp.

"I'm not the one who needs controlling," Lucia groused as she headed back up the hill.

———→

Dhanuk stalked through the undergrowth, careful not to make a sound. Finding a larger game trail, he examined the scat on the ground. *Deer. Good to know.* He followed the track down to a small waterfall, clambered up the slope and settled behind some huge rushes to spy on the broad pool at the head of the waterfall. Ducks bobbed on the surface, diving now and then for food. He nocked an arrow and quietly half rose. In seconds, he drew his bow and loosed, skewering a duck on the water. The rest of the flock took to the air, scattering even more birds in the trees. The fowl floated on the current and lodged between rocks at the top of the falls.

He stepped across the rock wall, and drew the duck from the water. On the other side of the pool, Dhanuk discovered more animal trails. Though narrower, this game trail was well travelled. He crouched behind several low bushes.

I'll set some traps along here. We should do well enough. I'll have to bring Ishir here. Show him how it's done. He held in a sigh. *I should be home. Talli will have had the babe before I return.* Grief at leaving his wife, loneliness at the prospect of months away, sat like a dark, angry crevasse inside him. *How long are we going to have to stay here?*

He rubbed his temple and waited, hoping the bitterness inside him would evaporate but only a dismal hole remained. Movement caught his eye and a hare hopped down the game trail. Oblivious to Dhanuk's presence, it grazed.

The hare stopped eating and its ears flicked back and forth, listening. Dhanuk drew his bow, lining up his target. A squeal rent the air. The hare bolted.

Dhanuk spun, trying to locate the sound's source.

He rose and stalked down the slopes toward the creek. Music filtered through the air, hauntingly beautiful, peaceful, alluring. It slowly filled the hole inside Dhanuk, and he halted, entranced. Curiosity aroused, he continued then stilled at the sound of children's voices.

Dhanuk crept forward through the undergrowth, downwind of the sounds. The music resumed. Peeking through ferns, Dhanuk spied a girl standing in a pond, peering at the water, while a boy sat on the bank playing a flute.

He looks like one of the refugees. The girl's one of us though. What are they doing out here? Hiding?

The boy on the embankment played the flute, and the music dominated Dhanuk's awareness, lulling him. He smiled. The tune held a soothing circular pattern; he felt warm and safe, and his eyes grew heavy. The girl's hands dived into the water and she pulled a large trout from the stream. As it wobbled, she toppled into the water and the fish hit the boy in the face. Dhanuk almost laughed.

One day Talli and I will have kids up to similar antics.

The music stopped. The peacefulness left Dhanuk, like a blanket ripped away.

He must be a kenati.

A great crashing came through the bushes and an attractive woman emerged pulling twigs from her curly, shoulder-length, brown hair.

Dhanuk's smiled. *They're in for it.*

Sure enough, the woman berated them and the two youngsters took off at a run.

He slid back and resumed his hunt.

CHAPTER THREE

DHANUK ENTERED THE CAMPSITE with a hare and the duck.

Parv and Ishir sat on logs before a small fire and had made sleeping pallets with pine needles as mattresses. The pile of firewood had grown, and a mound of mushrooms sat near a skillet.

They'd harvested a mass of long, straight, pine branches and had trimmed stakes to form walls for windbreaks.

"You've been busy," Dhanuk said.

"Well, there's no point in sitting on our arses," Parv said. "We could be here for a while; so, it might as well be comfortable." He motioned to the stakes. "We'll get the windbreaks up and then rebuild the shelter, make it bigger with timber walls. It'll be warmer when the cold sets in."

Dhanuk drew his dagger and sliced around the hare's legs and began skinning it in one piece. "By the gods, I hope we're out of here before winter."

"I've got no bloody idea, but now's the time to get it right," Parv said.

"It's a good spot," Ishir said. "Maybe we can come back here and use it as a hunting cabin?"

"Perhaps," Dhanuk said. "Though I reckon by the time it's done, I'll just be happy to be home with Talli and the babe. I'll not want to move again."

Parv laughed. "Turning into a family man."

"Yes. And happy to be so. My days of drinking and swiving any willing woman who comes my way are done. Talli is enough for me."

"Never thought I'd see the day." Parv shook his head. "You're goin' to miss out on a lot of fun."

Ishir grinned at Parv, idolisation clear in his gaze.

Dhanuk grimaced. *I'll have to inform that boy of a few facts about his hero, Parv. If I could have left Parv behind, I would have. I hope to gods he doesn't discover the woman and children.*

"Much sign of game?"

"Yes, deer, and these," he said, gesturing to his prizes. "Not much to up to west though, mostly lower down, where there's a bit more grass amongst the trees."

Parv frowned. "Not up west? Didn't we see a flock of ducks scatter to sky in that direction?"

"Maybe. There's a pool up there," Dhanuk said quickly. "That's where I got the ducks, but there's bugger all sign beyond that. Not worth the walk."

"Say, did you hear a weird kind of shriek?" Ishir asked.

Dhanuk paused in skinning the rabbit. "A shriek?" He shrugged. "I heard a shrieking owl, but there was nothing weird about it."

Parv stiffened, scrutinising him.

"An owl?" Ishir asked.

"Yes. You know, sometimes in these hills the sound bounces around a bit and can seem strange, but I didn't hear anything else."

Ishir looked at Parv, who raised his brows, but said nothing.

"I guess I'll check out the hunting tomorrow," Parv said, "when I take my turn at scrounging up dinner and you and Ishir can get more logs."

Dhanuk shrugged. "Sure, but I'd go east. You'll have better hunting."

→

Dhanuk tossed and turned, worry for the woman and children gnawed at him. Just before dawn, he rose and grabbed his bow. He looked at his other weapons and took only his dagger.

Ishir was asleep, but Parv stirred and groaned. "By the gods, what's got you roused out so early?"

Dhanuk sighed and ran his hands through his hair. "I spent the night worrying about Talli. I'm going for a walk. Maybe I'll find some more game, distract myself."

"She'll be fine." Parv chuckled. "Good wide hips on that one. You chose well. Beside your ma's had a dozen babes and still here."

Dhanuk's fist clenched around his bow. "Ma's had a dozen, but how many of them lived and how many saw her damn near die?"

Parv half rose and leaned on his elbow. "Ach! That was careless even for me. Look I'm sure she'll be fine and you'll be holding your son in no time. Go on, get lost for a bit and clear your head."

Dhanuk nodded, spun on his heel and left in the opposite direction from his previous trek. Before long he found a larger game trail. When he was far enough from their camp that Parv and Ishir wouldn't see where he'd gone, Dhanuk veered from the trail and headed up the mountain through the scrub. The hair on the back of his neck rose and the urge to turn tail gnawed at him. The farther he walked, the stronger the sensation of being watched grew. Once, he thought he saw movement farther up the ridge. He ducked behind a prickly box thorn, lay on his belly and peered at the ridge. Nothing. He strained to catch the sounds around him, hearing only the flutter of wings and a bright trill from a finch's nest nearby, yet he remained still, his breath shallow and quiet. There! At a break in the pines, a dark shape emerged from a copse of boxthorn and raised its head to pick leaves from a small stand of poplars. A doe and her fawn. *He's born late in the season. Well good luck to you little mother.* He watched them for a while.

"Gods, you're not wet behind the ears like Ishir. Act like a man." He rose and the pair bolted.

Dhanuk wove through the trees, nearing the small waterfall and pond. He crouched and moved forward under cover. Several ducks were already on the water. He aimed and loosed his arrow. The others took flight, squawking. Gathering his kill, he moved on hiking briskly over the mountainside. Finally spying a campsite below him. He froze. The woman and children were just getting up but surrounding them were a pack of Asena.

They're in danger! Wait... He studied the scene and noticed the children interacted with the creatures without fear. They actually talked to them and the Asena wagged their tails.

What's going on? Is it the boy kenati's doing?

He turned to leave but met the startling blue eyes of two Asena. He swallowed nervously, desperately fighting the instinct to reach for his dagger.

Legends say they're as intelligent as us. Dhanuk raised his hands, one held the duck's carcass. "I mean no harm. I saw them yesterday and worried they would struggle to feed themselves. I brought this," he said, waving the duck.

His heart drummed in his chest and sweat broke out on his brow.

"Who is it? Who's up there?" The woman's voice called.

The foremost Asena near Dhanuk flicked its gaze to the enormous beast standing below next to the woman. With a snap of its teeth, the group advanced on him, driving him down the slope toward the camp.

The largest Asena moved in front of the boy as Dhanuk entered the camp. His mother stood between the children with her arms resting on their shoulders.

"I'm not here to hurt anyone. I brought you this." Dhanuk put the duck on the ground. "I... I saw the children down by the pond the other day. I wasn't sure how you fared up here, so..."

The woman narrowed her eyes, hand squeezing the children's shoulders. "Thank you. We're doing well. We have ample help and protection."

"I can see that. If I'd known then—" He hesitated, glancing from the Asena, back to her. He drew a sharp breath. "I... I didn't just come to offer food. I also hoped you'd be moving on. You see, there are three of us. We've deserted Ratilal's army. We just want to wait out the war up here and return home safe, but I don't want Parv to know about you."

"Parv?"

"One of the other scouts. He's not... not a good man. Even with the Asena, you should move on."

"We will. We've plenty of protection. You should leave."

Dhanuk nodded. "I... I won't tell them." His gaze shifted to the boy. "Are you a kenati?"

The boy stood tall and puffed out his chest. "I will be."

"Your music is wonderful." Dhanuk eyed the Asena, anxiously; rubbed his sweaty palms on his pants. "I hope to hear you when your training is finished." Dhanuk's voice quavered. "Is... is she the Matriarch?"

"Yes," the girl said.

Dhanuk went down on one knee. "Greetings, old mother. I mean no harm." The Matriarch snarled at him, and the Asena closed around the family. Dhanuk tensed as he fought the urge to bolt from the campsite. He left the duck and backed away. "I'll leave. I won't be back, but you should move on. Stay this high for a good while or you might run into the others."

Dhanuk's path returned him to the mountain pond. His pulse slowed the farther he travelled from them. Each glance over his shoulder revealed nothing but trees and rocks. He had to return to the others from the same direction he'd left, but he needed to catch something to bring to camp. *Deer maybe.* He knelt beside the water, said a prayer and took a drink, heaving a sigh of relief. Dhanuk crossed the pond wall and hit the deer trail again. The track descended the slope, winding between a boulder outcrop. He exited the shadow of the rocks and slammed to a halt. The Matriarch stood on the track before him. He spun. An Asena leapt from the boulder, hit him in the chest and knocked him to the ground. His head collided with a rock and his world went black.

The Matriarch sniffed the body, curled her lip and tore out his throat.

CHAPTER FOUR

PIO'S STOMACH RUMBLED. "MA, I'm hungry. Is there anything to eat?"

"No. Your fish is gone and the duck is gone. We ate it all last night."

"Kiriz and I can go back to the stream and get another fish. It'll be easy."

"No! You'll just have to wait. I'm sure the Asena will bring us something when the rest of them return."

Pio glanced to the two smaller Asena who remained with them. "Where do you think the others went?"

"I suspect it has something to do with the man who came by," Lucia said. "They're probably just making sure we're safe." The colour drained from her face and her mouth twisted as if it tasted something bitter. Lucia rubbed her back. "Gods, another day in the saddle!"

Pio scuffed the ground and kicked a rock into the distance.

Kiriz sat on a nearby log, watching him with a grin. "Are you bored?"

"Aren't you?"

Fiamma let out two high chirps from her perch in a nearby tree.

Kiriz laughed. "Hey, I think Fiamma just agreed with me. You could play some music." Her eyes darted toward Lucia. "Maybe something that might help Lucia's aches."

"I don't know if I can do that," Pio said.

"You could try," Kiriz said. "Do what you did with the fish only think about soothing your ma's aches so she's nice and relaxed. *Really* relaxed."

Lucia glanced at Kiriz, eyes narrowed, frowning at the girl's tone.

Kiriz smiled innocently. "It'll make her day easier." Kiriz moved behind him.

"You can try if you like, Pio," his mother said.

Pio picked up his flute and put it to his lips. The tune commenced brightly and he focused his will on his mother, first concentrating on where he'd seen her rub her back. His melody morphed from bright and bouncy to slow, relaxed, almost wistful, but he visualised it swirling around her, entering her stiff muscles and joints, chasing away her aches and pains.

Lucia sat on her bedroll and lay back. "It's working. Keep going."

Pio's eyes twinkled as he continued and Lucia let out a long sigh. She closed her eyes and drifted into a deep sleep. His gaze flicked to the two young Asena, who investigated Lucia's sleeping form. Pio transformed the tune into a cyclical lullaby; low tones wafted from the flute and floated around the trio. The two young Asena curled beside his mother, closed their eyes and slept. Pio faded the tune out and rose slowly. Fiamma glided to a rock and canted her head, scrutinising the sleeping trio. She turned to face Pio, her dark eyes unblinking. He lowered his head, unable to meet her gaze.

"Let's go," Kiriz whispered. "Let's get breakfast. I'm starving and it'll surprise her when she wakes. We might even get three fish and give some to the Asena."

They ran down to the creek, Fiamma flitting ahead of them. Kiriz pulled off her boots and rolled up her pant legs then waded into the pool. "Okay, start playing." She grinned maniacally. "I'm ready!"

Pio sat on the bank and played the same tune he had the day before. Nothing. "Maybe that was the only fish here."

"Let's follow the creek downhill for a bit and see if there's another pond," Kiriz said.

Pio glanced back the way they'd travelled. "We probably shouldn't go far. What about the strangers?"

Kiriz snorted. "Them? The Asena have fixed them! Who would come and attack if they knew we had a pack of Asena with us? No one would." She climbed out of the creek and put on her boots. "Come on."

The pair hiked down the mountain, sticking close to the creek as it wended its way through and around boulder outcrops. As they descended, the surrounding trees shifted from conifers to a mix of beech and ash. They stopped at a large pool surrounded by weeping birch trees. Their pale bark was a balm after the dark, straight pines.

Kiriz peered into the pool. "I think it's deeper than the other one." She picked up a fallen branch and dipped it into the water, measuring the depth. "Too deep."

"Try over there, where those rocks pile up," Pio said.

Kiriz clambered over and through the canopy of a fallen tree and tested the water depth near a pile of rock that had tumbled into the pool when the tree fell from higher up the mountain. "It should be just up to my knees."

She doffed her boots and climbed in. "Ow! They're pointy."

"Don't cut yourself. Ma will lose her marbles."

"Gods! You worry as much as she does! Just play your flute."

———▶

Parv dropped the last pine log between the stakes and stepped back to survey their work. Two log walls stood as wind breaks before their makeshift tent and cooking area. He and Ishir had cut more logs to make cabin walls.

"Don't you think he should've been back by now?"

"He's skiving off work. Or feeling bloody sorry for himself thinking about your sister. Hunting my arse! He'd better come back with deer at least."

"He will," Ishir said. "And he said he'd be here to help."

"Well, I'm done for the day. We'll wait until he can help. Let him do some of the work."

Ishir gathered his weapons. "I'm going to look for him."

Parv sighed. "No. You stay here and I'll go. You might get lost or miss signs of his trail."

Ishir's shoulders slumped. "I'm not useless, you know. I could find him."

"Of course you could, ordinarily, but tracking in this terrain is bloody difficult. Give yourself a couple more years and you'll be doing it easily."

"You could teach me?"

"Not today."

Parv donned his weapons and headed out to find Dhanuk. This deep into the forest, Dhanuk had clearly been unafraid of being tracked by the enemy, and Parv found enough traces of his trail to follow him through the rocky terrain. He halted where the trail branched, noticed deer scat and took the lower trail. The rocky path wended its way down the mountain, and Parv spotted a footprint in muddy soil near a spring that was seeping across the track, so he continued between a large outcrop of boulders. Abruptly, he stopped and his breath hitched. Keeping his body hidden in the shadows of the rock, he stared at the body of Dhanuk.

A chill ran down his spine and he scrutinised his surroundings. Sword drawn, he walked to the body and knelt by the blood pool. It had barely congealed. Within the bloody dirt lay the enormous paw print. *Asena*. He looked back the way he'd come and thought about Ishir.

No. Not going back there yet. Our scent will be strongest around there. Was it the Asena Dhanuk didn't want us to see? Why? Gods, if he'd known, he would have said and we'd be gone. Must be something else he didn't want us to know. Something in the west.

Parv moved back along the track to where it split. Examining the game trail, he followed it up the mountain. Part way along he found the trace of a footprint. *So, he came this way.* Parv continued and paused at the pond. On a hunch, he crossed the rock wall, peered at the soil, seeking signs of Dhanuk's passage before moving on.

Upon a rocky outcrop, he stopped and stared down into a campsite where he saw a woman sleeping and two Asena. *Sleeping with them? Is she kenati? She can't be. She looks like one of those refugees. They really are pale as milk. The Asena must have killed Dhanuk to protect her. Only two of them. No one's seen Asena here in generations.* A quiver of doubt ran through him. *They're sacred. Leave them be.*

The thought of Dhanuk's mauled body stayed in his mind. *He would never have hurt them, or even offered insult to them. Look what they did. No one deserved to die like that.* For all Parv knew, the myths were wrong, or they'd changed. *But there's the woman? Next, it'll be me. No way! It's just two.*

His lips twisted into a smile. He judged the breeze and backtracked, descending the slope to enter the camp downwind. Spying from between two shrubs, he saw no sign of anyone else. He drew his bow and let loose a volley of arrows. Two yelps pierced the air. The woman woke in fright, screamed, and scrambled to her feet. Parv charged and attacked the wounded Asena who struggled to rise.

He slashed his sword down across its head and neck, rending its flesh. The Asena collapsed in a pool of blood. Pain erupted across his back. He staggered, spun, to find the woman holding a thick branch before her. Parv knocked it from her hands. He punched her in the face and she collapsed.

Parv walked to the second Asena and nudged it with his boot. Nothing. He scanned the camp for anything useful; found little.

He sheathed his sword and hauled the woman to her feet. "You're coming with me."

CHAPTER FIVE

PIO BEGAN THE SAME calming cycle he'd played the day before and Kiriz stood eagerly in the water, waiting for her chance to catch breakfast.

Eyes wide, she looked at Pio. "That wasn't a fish," she whispered.

He kept playing, willing her to stay in the water. *There's no way we're missing breakfast again.*

Kiriz trembled as she watched the dark water. She shuddered. "I want to get out."

Pio continued to focus on her. *Stay, catch. Stay, catch!* The tune held its pattern.

Kiriz remained rooted to the spot. "Pio, what are you doing?" She was pale, her hands shook above the water. "There it is again!"

She's being such a girl!

Kiriz let out a squeal. "It bit me! It's got me!"

Pio stopped playing and Kiriz leapt out of the water with a crayfish attached to her big toe. She hopped over the rocks, shaking her foot, but the cray held on. Pio scrambled over fallen branches to reach her.

"Stop dancing about! You'll lose it!"

"I want to lose it! It hurts! Get it off me!"

He knelt, grabbed her leg with one hand and the lobster in the other. He pulled.

"Ow! Not like that!"

Pio broke a small stick off a nearby branch and jabbed the cray with it. The creature let go of her and latched onto the stick. Kiriz sat and rubbed her bruised and cut toe. She winced as she wiggled it.

"Well done!" Pio said. "River crays are yum!"

Kiriz shoved him with her uninjured foot. "And how are we going to cook it? We haven't got any pots to boil it in."

The grin slipped from Pio's face. "You're right. Can't we just put it on a stick over the flames, or in the coals?" He held the crayfish's carapace behind its white claws, which snapped at the air, and examined it's black, shiny shell and white spikes. "Ma, will figure it out."

"I don't know. We won't get much off it. We'll need more."

"Yep. Hop back in. We'll try for more."

"What! With my toes as bait! No way!"

Pio wouldn't meet her eyes. "Mmm... they look different at home," he said and put the cray back into the water.

Kiriz watched him, outrage boiling across her face. She put on her socks and boots and stormed off.

"Hey! Wait up!" He caught up with her. "Why're you so mad?"

"You know why!" She shoved him. "I'm not bait! And you did something to me! Me! I wanted to get out of the water, but I couldn't. It was like I couldn't move my own legs!"

Pio gaped. "Really? All I thought was how I wanted you to stay still and catch something. I didn't think it would do that."

She narrowed her eyes at him. "Well, what did you think it would do?"

He shrugged, looking away. "Just kind of give you a suggestion to stay? I don't really know."

"Well, it didn't! It was horrible not being able to get out! I was really scared! How would you like it if you wanted to run and couldn't."

"I wouldn't, but I knew there wouldn't be anything that could really hurt you."

"What! Is that all you can say?"

Pio rolled his eyes. "You're being silly."

Red faced, Kiriz marched toward him and poked him in the chest. "Silly! I couldn't move. You knew that!" She stood hands fisted, red faced. "You knew what your magic was doing and you didn't care. That's what an evil magician would do. Just like the ones you told me about."

Evil? The word lingered in his mind, tendrils rooting there. "I..." He hung his head. *Evil.* "I...I didn't think. I...I guess...You're right. I'm sorry, Kiriz. I won't do that again—"

A scream ripped through the air.

"Ma!"

The pair of them raced through the forest back to camp. They pounded up the mountainside, scrambling over fallen logs and darting between boulders. Kiriz slipped on pine needles. Pio hauled her to her feet. Lungs heaving, they pushed on until, legs burning with strain, they drew closer to the campsite.

Kiriz grabbed Pio and hauled him back. "No. Wait," she whispered, dragging him behind the bole of a large pine. Panic stricken, Pio tried to shrug her off, but she held tight. "We've got to be smart. Slow down, be quiet."

Hunched, they stole forward to the edge of the campsite. From behind cover they saw Lucia fighting a brawny man. She kicked, wriggled, slapped or punched him wherever she could.

"We have to stop him," Pio whispered.

"Yes, but let's not charge in there. Think. We'll only get one chance. We haven't got any weapons."

Kiriz's gaze darted around and she grabbed a long stick. Pio stared at her standing before him – short, wiry, frightened eyes belying the fierce look on her face. He looked at the hulk of a man fighting his mother.

Crazy. Kiriz will die. So will I. No weapons. What can we do?

Lucia screamed as the man slapped her. She spun sideways, stumbled, and her head hit a rock.

Ma!

"Pio, your flute! Use your flute!" Kiriz whispered, harshly.

Pio stared dumbly at it.

"Make him stand still and I'll bash him on the head!"

Pio bit his lip, fear churning his guts. *I have a weapon. Gods help me.*

The man nudged Lucia with his foot. She was unconscious. "Damn you! You're too much trouble! I'm done with you!" He prepared to draw his sword.

A white-hot anger surged within Pio. It burned the last remnants of the impish, happy-go-lucky boy to shreds until innocence hung like a tattered rag around him and all that remained was wildness and fury.

Pio shrugged Kiriz off and ran into the clearing. "Stop!"

The warrior sneered and took a step toward Pio, drew his sword. "Just what are you going to do to stop me?"

He advanced.

"I said stop!" Pio yelled.

"Ooo! I'm scared!" The man drew closer.

Pio put his flute to his lips and the man threw his head back and laughed.

Rage filled Pio. He blew one long, deep note on his flute. The crystals in his pocket thrummed in reply. *Stop!*

The man went to take another step but couldn't. The mocking grin fell from his face. "What have you done? Release me!"

Kiriz leapt from cover. "No." She swung her branch at his head. He ducked, grabbed the branch and yanked it from her. He swung it knocking her off her feet.

"Boy, you let me go now if you know what's good for you!"

Kiriz scrambled to her feet. "No! If he lets you go, you'll hurt us all."

Pio's refrain, low and full of simmering hate, circled his mother's attacker, binding him.

"I won't. I'll leave." His calculating gaze never left the pair as he edged his hand to his dagger. "I've seen your power. I'll leave." His fingers tightened around the hilt.

In a flash, he hurled the dagger at Pio.

Pio dived sideways, forcing all his frenzied fear and wrath into a screeching high note. *No! Stop!*

Kiriz winced, covered her ears, fell to the ground and curled up. Pio barely noticed her, focusing all his will on his mother's assailant.

The man staggered forward and clutched his chest.

A shrill cry from above, and Fiamma dove from the sky, attacking the enemy's face. He dropped his sword and flailed, knocking her aside. She hit the dirt, shook herself and took to the air.

Fiamma, stay away! Pio ordered, continuing to blast the deadly, piercing note.

The warrior, eyes wide, gulped air like a dying fish. Beads of sweat dotted his forehead. Veins stood out on his neck. His face twisted in pain and he turned puce as he reached for Pio — struggling with each gasp to rip the flute from him.

Pio remained rooted to the spot, his notes growing more strident as the man staggered like he was wading through a bog; each step a herculean, excruciatingly slow effort.

Stop! Stop! NO! STOP! NOW! Pio thought. Horrified, eyes wide, trembling, he watched as fingers closed around the end of the flute. They gripped. Pio's breath faltered and the last note trailed hopelessly off. The flute tore from his fingers as the man collapsed, dead, at his feet.

Shaking, Pio cast his eyes down. The man still gripped his flute.

Pio wrenched his flute from the soldier's hands and, clutching it to his chest, staggered back. His heart drummed in his ears. Looking around for Kiriz, he saw her unmoving on the ground. Pio's vision took on an orange hue and blurred. He fell to his knees. *They're all dead. I killed them all.* Sweat beaded his brow and a shiver ran along his spine before he shook all over. He turned from the sight of the bodies crumpled around him, fell to his knees and vomited.

Pio wiped his mouth. An anguished knot of grief gripped him. He wrapped his arms around his middle and rocked himself back and forth, eyes tightly closed. A long low, visceral keen built within him tearing its way into the world and ending on a harsh wail that ripped through the air. "No-no-no-no-no..." He curled upon himself, face in his hands.

Fiamma flew to him, landing on his shoulder. She trilled softly at him. Pio whimpered. She bit his ear.

"Ow!" Pio snapped his head up and rubbed his ear. Fiamma let out a string of high chirps and darted to Kiriz, who moaned.

"Kiriz!" Pio scrambled over to her. "Kiriz, are you all right?" He wrapped his arms around her.

"Yes, my chest felt tight and..." She put her hands to her ears. "It's a wonder my ears aren't bleeding. That was the worst noise I've heard."

"I'm so glad you're all right! I-I... I'm sorry!"

"Check your ma," Kiriz said, drawing a shuddering breath as she sat up.

Pio ran to Lucia. "Ma! Ma!"

Blood ran from a cut on her temple, and Pio leaned close to her face. "She's breathing!" He shook her gently. "Ma? Wake up."

Nothing.

Kiriz joined him. Together, they sat there, staring at her.

"We should do something," Kiriz whispered. She darted off to the pile of gear and saddles waiting to put on the horses.

Tears streamed down Pio's face. Fiamma landed on his shoulder, chirping quietly, canting her head at him. He stroked her. "Thanks, girl."

Kiriz returned with their bedrolls and a water flask. She covered Lucia with a blanket and put another, folded one under her head then passed the flask to Pio. "Bathe the cut on her face."

Pio tore a corner off his shirt and wet it, before dabbing it on the wound. As the blood washed away, it revealed the cut was not large, but a bruise was forming along her cheekbone.

"We need some bandages," he said.

"I'll check the saddlebags." Kiriz ran to the gear stash and rummaged through the saddlebags. She pulled out a bandage and a small, glazed jar. Kiriz removed the stopper, sniffed it and dipped her finger into the jar, peering at the salve on her finger. She gasped in surprise and raced back to Pio.

"Look what I found! I think it's honeygold and duckweed. This stops bleeding."

"Are you sure?" Pio said, staring at the disgusting mixture.

"Almost."

"But what if it makes her worse?"

"I don't think anything bad would be put with the medic kit. It can't hurt."

Pio nodded and Kiriz smoothed the ointment on Lucia's wound. Pio tore another section off his shirt, which he folded and placed over the gash. Together, they bandaged Lucia's head.

Fiamma, leapt off a log and took to the air with a screech. She arrowed between the trees in the forest and circled back, chirruping rapidly as she alighted on a branch.

The Matriarch and the other adult Asena burst out of the bushes, their fur bloodied. The Matriarch loped to the fallen Asena, sniffing their bodies and frantically nudging them with her nose. The pack surrounded the bodies, hunched, heads low, tails hanging low, scenting the blood. Whines filled the air. The Matriarch sat on her haunches and howled. The pack joined in and the eerie chorus reverberated throughout the forest.

Pio's wail joined theirs as he sobbed uncontrollably. Kiriz burst into tears.

When their howls subsided, the Asena lay slumped next to the bodies. The Matriarch turned from the grieving pack and approached Lucia, whined and nudged her. She licked first Pio, then Kiriz on the face. Pio wrapped his arms around her and buried his face in her fur. When his sobs faded, she sat and stared at him.

Pio hung his head. His stomach churned and nausea roiled through him. He scuttled back from her, drew his knees up to his chest, wrapped his arms around them and hid his face from view. *Oh Gods! I did this!* He mumbled a prayer. "Majula, Ariceli help me! *No! That's not right! They won't hear me. Not here.* "Rana, Jalal please help me! Forgive me! Make them forgive me. I killed my friends... and Ma —" He moaned. *What if she never wakes up?* Pio trembled and hugged himself harder, his breathing ragged.

The Matriarch nudged him.

"This is our fault."

Her ears pricked forward and Pio felt an unfamiliar nudge against his mind. "No," he whispered. "No, don't look." He tried to scoot away again, and his muscles froze as an iron band wrapped around him. Pio looked up, tears streaming down his face. "Please, don't."

The Matriarch rammed his mind demanding entrance. Pio quailed before her will. He knew she could probably invade his thoughts no matter what he did, and this was the most polite she would be. Ashamed, he let her in. She riffled through his memories, focussing on Pio putting Lucia and the Asena to sleep.

The Matriarch snapped a hair's breadth from his face. He didn't flinch.

She stalked the campsite, inhaling all the surrounding scents, tracing the children's steps out of the clearing. She lunged toward Pio and snapped, before continuing her pacing, growling all the while.

Finally, she approached him, her lip curled. She stared into his eyes. Pio looked away and she bit his hand. He cradled his injury but met her gaze; concentrated on her. An image popped into his mind of a man leading a string of mules carrying a group of children.

Hamza. "The Matriarch thinks we need to find Hamza," Pio said to Kiriz.

"How are we going to do that? The forest is huge."

"Fiamma can find them."

Pio looked at his guardian perched in a nearby pine. *Find Hamza,* Pio thought at her, along with a mental image of the mule train. Fiamma joined minds with him and took flight.

He felt Fiamma's wings beat as she gained height. By the time she captured an up-draft and soared high above the trees, he was one with her. Their wings flapped lazily as she soared the air currents. They scanned the forest for signs of movement and increased their search area. Nothing.

Time vanished. Fiamma veered east, flying towards Haverrac's Gate and The Stairs of the Gods, which marked the entrance to Hamza's home in the ancient caldera. Nothing. They backtracked and their sharp eyes scanned the lower slopes of the Bear Tooth Mountains. Having passed the point at which the camp lay, they continued to scan the country toward the Four Ways Lake.

Travelling with a bunch of little kids probably made him slower than us.

Endless trees and rocks lay underneath them, but no Hamza.

Rounding a slope, Fiamma gave a long cry and dived. There amongst the bare oaks and birch, whose golden leaves were gracing the ground, they saw movement.

As she swooped low, the train of mules, bobbing their heads, came into full view. Fiamma returned to the camp, swooping low and releasing her hold on Pio.

Pio stiffened and gritted his teeth as a sense of falling rushed over him. He shaded his eyes and blinked rapidly as he returned to his senses. "We found them." He tried to picture the place in his mind, but the Matriarch turned her back on him and faced Fiamma, who alighted on a log.

"What's happening?" Kiriz asked.

"I'm not sure. I think Fiamma is showing them where Hamza is." Pio's eyes welled up. "The Matriarch is mad at me. Really mad."

"I'm pretty sure she's mad at *us*. It was my idea remember."

The Matriarch turned a withering gaze upon her and bared her teeth. Kiriz slumped. "I'm sorry. If we'd known —"

The Matriarch touched noses with the second largest Asena, who lowered his head, wagged his tail and vanished into the forest. Fiamma followed him.

Kiriz rose and the Matriarch snarled at her. "I just want another water bottle," she said.

The Asena nearest Kiriz shoved her with its muzzle, until she sat. Another Asena dropped a water flask at the girl's feet. The Matriarch eyeballed the children and then the Asena encircled them and lay down to sleep.

Kiriz clutched Pio's hand as the pair eyed the mass of Asena trapping them.

CHAPTER SIX

PIO AWOKE, RED EYED, to the jingle of a harness through the trees. He rubbed his eyes and sat up. Hamza entered the clearing on his mule.

The cordon of Asena around Pio and Kiriz, parted to admit Hamza and an Asena. Fiamma landed in the branch of a tree and chirruped at Pio.

"Well, about time I found you," Hamza said, dismounting. "Morning, old mother," he said to The Matriarch. "That damn bird, wouldn't give me a moment's peace. Anytime I stopped for a rest, she'd swoop me and squawk like an outraged mumma until I got movin' again." He drew his reins through the bridle throat lash and then looped them over the stirrup, leaving his mule to graze. "You're in a right state, aren't you?"

Pio stared at him, exhausted, dazed; mute. A haze clouded Pio's mind and lethargy sat like chains around him. He struggled to raise his head. Hamza leaned down and cupped Pio's chin and stared into his eyes. "You in there, boy?" Rainbow lightning danced across Hamza's eyes and vanished.

Pio pulled away, shook his head, then blinked and rubbed his eyes. "Uh... yes."

"Mmm, still waking up, I reckon." Hamza opened his saddlebags, tossed Pio an apple, and ripped a small loaf of bread in half before passing a section to Pio. "Eat."

Kiriz woke and grinned. "Hamza!"

"Here, young Kiriz," he said, tossing an apple and the other half of the loaf to her. "Get that into you. Girl, what have you got yourself into this time? We rode past a campsite down there and there's blood and guts from one end of it to the other."

"Blood and guts?" Kiriz said. "Oh! That must be the other soldier. Some of the Asena left us the other day and came back all bloody."

"Mmm, well they made short work of whoever was there," he said, kneeling beside Lucia. "This your ma, boy?" Pio nodded. "What's happened to her?"

Pio's voice rasped. "A deserter from Ratilal's army attacked her. She hit her head and she won't wake up."

Hamza examined the wound. "Looks like you did a right good bit of tending to it. Nothing I can improve on there, but we'll just have to figure out a way to wake her up."

Pio stared at his ma despondently, the food in his lap forgotten.

"Now, boy..."

"His name's Pio," Kiriz said around a mouthful of apple.

"Pio, right then. Eat up. You'll need your strength." Hamza shoved the apple under Pio's nose. "Eat!"

Pio bit into the apple, and sweet, tangy, juice filled his mouth. His stomach grumbled and, despite his misery, he devoured it and felt brighter with each mouthful.

Hamza checked Lucia for any other injuries. As he worked, he said, "You two were meant to be on my mule train with the others and you buggered off into the woods to have fun, didn't you?" His gaze captured Pio and pinned him. A shiver ran down Pio's spine. "You two been wandering off again, or somethin'?"

Pio and Kiriz stopped eating and looked at each other, before eying the Asena and the stone cairn.

Hamza studied them. "Right, one of you tell me what happened from the beginning."

Pio, head bowed, said nothing.

Kiriz watched him, food forgotten, her eyes welling with tears. "All right." She related their tale to Hamza. Gradually, Pio looked up, adding details here and there, while he observed the old man as Kiriz spoke.

He doesn't seem surprised. Not one bit.

Kiriz fell silent, her eyes shining with tears; she gazed at Hamza expectantly.

He walked to the Matriarch and sat beside her, one hand resting in her fur. Hamza bowed his head. Goosebumps broke out on Pio's skin. The hairs on the backs of his arms rose and he felt a current around him. Yet, when he looked at the trees, the branches were still.

They waited for Hamza to speak, yet the entire world was silent—trapped in the same grave repose as the Matriarch and the muleteer.

The children glanced at each other. Hope fled Kiriz's face, her expression dimmed. Pio wept.

At the sound of his sniffles, Hamza looked up. "Enough of that now, young Pio."

"It's all my fault," he said.

Hamza returned to their sides. "How so?"

"We didn't do as we were told. If we'd stayed here, then the first man wouldn't have seen us."

"True, but he didn't hurt you. In fact, he offered you food. And from what Kiriz said, I don't think he would've told the others." He shook his head. "No, the fellow that slayed the young 'uns found your camp on his own."

"But we weren't here when he came!" Pio yelled, hands fisted. He sagged. "We weren't here. We should have been. We could have stopped him."

"What? You two? How? You didn't even know what you could do then." Hamza waved the idea away. "And even if you had, do you think your power would work in time to stop him when he's got arrow ready to fly?" Pio opened his mouth to speak, but Hamza went on. "No. You'd both be dead. The Asena would still probably have died and he'd have run off with your ma."

"I... No. We should never have left," Pio said.

"He's right, Pio," Kiriz said.

"'Course I'm right," Hamza said with a chuckle. "Now, Pio, let's see if we can wake up your ma."

"We've tried and tried."

"Ah, but did you try your music?"

Pio gaped. "No! No, I can't. Bad things happen!"

"Not always. Your music does what you want and it bends the Wild to your will."

Pio averted his eyes.

"Ach, now. Think back. I'm sure old Umniga would've told you about the Wild. It's also called the flumenatiat."

"A bit, but we didn't get far before—"

"Before the enemy killed her," Hamza said with a sigh.

Pio and Kiriz both nodded.

"Well, what you did to that man – your music, your will asked the question and the Wild answered."

"Just like that?"

"Mostly, yes."

Pio peered at Hamza's face as lightening flared in his eyes and vanished with a blink.

Pio rubbed his eyes and squinted at Hamza, seeing nothing but smiling eyes and wrinkles.

"You, all right, boy? You look like you'll keel over."

Hamza placed his hand on Pio's shoulder. "Think about the great things you've done with your music. I mean, you tethered Isa when she was ill and you helped recall her."

"How do you know that?" Pio asked.

Hamza frowned. "Er... I reckon someone told me or I heard it." He rushed on. "I mean news of the first bard kenati, probably the greatest, in generations gets around."

Pio shook his head. "Greatest bard kenati? I'll never be that. I killed someone when I just wanted him to stop and I hurt Kiriz – I made her do something she didn't want. And—" He hung his head.

Hamza leaned close to him. "And?"

Pio's breath shuddered and he turned so Kiriz couldn't see his face. "I thought '*stop*' again and again, but he kept coming." Pio's wrung his hands. "I was really scared and I wanted him to... to just *end*... to die."

Hamza sighed. "You did your best to defend your Ma and yourself. Killing is not good, but sometimes defending those we love we must do it. Your pa is off fighting with Karan's warriors, he'll kill to defend those he loves - they all will."

Pio fidgeted, scuffing the dirt with his toes. "I don't want to do it ever again."

"That's good. Gods willing you won't have to."

"But you don't know and I thought Kiriz was being a whimp, I didn't care that she was scared," he whispered.

"I see, but Pio you're sorry you did those things to Kiriz. Will you do them again?

"No! Um...I hope not, but the music gets inside me and... the Wild... The *magic* felt good – like I could do anything I wanted."

"Ah, well, that may never go away, but you know bard kenati used to teach lore and tell tales. They brought joy.

They were never warriors." Hamza gave a long sigh. "You will be the only one. You'll travel all of Altaica and tell stories, sing songs. You will be welcomed at nearly every hearth. You will bring joy. You'll have years of training in lore and tales and you can practise and learn control."

"What if I can't?"

"You saved Isa," Hamza said.

"Only because Umniga and all the kenati were there and the Asena."

"Umniga would not have wanted you there unless your music was very important to that ritual. I think *you* are why it worked."

"Really?"

"Yes." Hamza put the flute in his hands. "Come on then, give it a go."

Pio sat beside his mother.

"Think of your ma and how much you want her back. Think only of that, of her getting well and waking up."

The moment Pio put the flute near his mouth, all the Asena, apart from the Matriarch, left. Kiriz and Hamza sat side by side, and the Matriarch joined them.

Pio began haltingly. Notes stuttering from the flute like tear drops.

"Think on your ma. How much you miss her. How much you want her to return, nothing else," Hamza whispered. He undid the bandage around Lucia's head, exposing the gash on her temple.

The tune slid sadly forth and transformed into melancholic joy as Pio remembered all the adventures, the fun, little things from life back home in Penīdīen. Images of his father and mother, laughing, hugging; his mother chasing Pio to catch and tickle him... all of it poured forth into his music."

Lucia's fingers twitched.

Pio's music stuttered.

"Keep going, lad." Hamza sat close; a warm, comforting presence. A sense of safety filled Pio; for once, as if everything would be fine. The tune redoubled. Pio looked at the cut on his mother's face and thought about the tear as if it were a garment that needed stitching. He envisioned the ragged edges joining, sealing, becoming smooth, unblemished skin again.

Hamza drew a harsh intake of breath as the wound closed.

Pio, buoyed, produced a melody that capered around his mother, trilling high and low, and teasingly like a bratty child calling, 'Ma! Ma! Ma! Come back!'

Lucia's eyes fluttered open.

Pio dropped his flute. "Ma!" He leaned down and hugged her.

"Oof! Pio. Whatever's wrong?" Lucia's eyes widened, she gasped and sat up, her gaze darting around the campsite. "Where is he?"

"Ma, it's all right. Fiamma found Hamza. She and the Asena brought him here."

"Hamza? Oh!"

"Yes, the other one is dead," said Pio.

"And gone," said Kiriz. "The Asena dragged him off."

"We're safe?"

"Yep."

"Thank the gods!" Lucia leaned forward, her head in her hands. "Oh! My head! I feel... I think..." She turned sideways and retched. "I'm so dizzy."

"Lie still," Hamza said. "That's it, just curl up. Kiriz, get me a water flask." Kiriz darted to him, handing him a flask. "When you can, Lucia, sit up slowly." Lucia moaned and lay panting for a few minutes before inching onto her elbow, head hung. Hamza knelt behind her and helped her sit. He held the flask to her lips. "Drink."

Lucia sipped the water then wiped her mouth. "Thank goodness you arrived, Hamza. Thank you for saving us."

"It was all over when I got here," Hamza said. "Young Pio saved the day."

"Pio!" She stared at her son, aghast. "How?"

Pio refused to meet her gaze.

Kiriz frowned at him. "Pio, you did a good thing."

Jaw clenched, arms folded, Pio stared into the distance.

"Pio?" Lucia asked.

Nothing.

"He called upon the Wild to help him, and it did," Hamza said.

"The Wild?"

Pio snuck a look at his mother. He didn't think she could become any paler, but all colour drained from her.

"Like, Isa," Lucia whispered.

"Magic, Ma. I used magic," Pio said, drawing his knees up to his chin and hiding his face from her. "Don't hate me."

"Hate you?" Lucia said. "How could I hate you?"

"You hated Isa when she got magic."

"I... I didn't... hate her," Lucia said. "I was frightened, Pio. During the Great War back home, mages caused devastation." She hesitated, reaching out to him, but dropped her hand. "I'm sure they did good too, but we only remember the bad. Kiriz is right. Saving me was a good thing. That man had evil in his heart and you stopped him, no matter how you did it."

Pio peeked at her. His voice was thick with tears. "Really?"

"Yes." Lucia held open her arms. "Come here." Pio rushed into her embrace. "You're my son. I'll always love you."

Pio trembled as he clung to his mother and she rubbed his back. "Ma, you're shaking!" He sat back and looked at her.

"Lie down a while longer, Lucia," Hamza said. He rose, grabbed their blankets and covered Lucia with them. "It's all right, Pio. She's been through a lot. We'll just give her time to rest and she will be fine. Kiriz, you sit beside Lucia while Pio shows me to the pond so I can water my mule." He rose, unfurled his mount's reins. "Come on, Pio."

Pio looked anxiously at his mother. "Kiriz can show you."

"I want you to show me."

Pio froze at the timbre of Hamza's voice. It pierced him, bone deep.

"Off you go, Pio. I'll be fine." His mother smiled at him. She didn't seem to notice anything amiss.

"I've got her, Pio," Kiriz said.

He turned by inches and looked at Hamza, who stood, brow quirked, grinning at him. "Come on, poor Mika here is thirsty," he said, rubbing the mule's brow.

Pio rose, frowning. "This way."

Hamza and the Matriarch followed behind Pio. A shudder ran through Pio and he jogged through the trees. He was torn between the need to bolt and not to take his eyes off the man - bolting won. Finally, they reached the pond. Pio halted, allowing Hamza to come alongside him, but Pio kept his distance.

"What's eating you, eh?"

Pio's mouth grew dry. It's Hamza. Isa trusts Hamza. She trusts him. He drew a deep breath, flinched, and took half a step back. "Your voice. There was something funny about your voice."

Hamza threw his head back and laughed. "You're not the only one with a bit of magic in you, boy."

Pio gaped.

"Ach, don't be fretting about it. Sometimes it comes to me on the voice of the goddess." He sat on a rock by the water's edge and watched his mule drink greedily. The Matriarch curled up and rested her head on Hamza's foot. "Sit down, Pio. We can take a bit of time."

Goddess? The goddess showed us where to find the crystal. Wide eyed, Pio sat cross-legged in the dirt and gazed up at Hamza. "Will Ma really be fine?"

Hamza nodded. "Though she'll have sore head for a few days. We'll get her down the mountain and to the mule train by tonight. Then she can rest and we'll begin our trek home again tomorrow or the next day." Pio nodded. Hamza pointed his finger at him. "But, young Pio, I want a word with you. You *forgot* to tell me something earlier."

"Forgot?" Pio scratched his head.

"Yes. We need to have a talk about those flame-eye crystals in your pocket."

Pio blanched. "Um. Isa said I shouldn't tell anyone."

"I already know about them, so I think you're in the clear on that one."

"Er—"

"What did they do when you played your flute?"

"They... they vibrated and got warm."

"Did they now? Interesting. Tell me, how did you feel, Pio, when you killed that warrior?"

"Relieved. Scared but sick. Really sick, like I could've thrown up. I don't want to do that again, ever."

Hamza rubbed his chin and sat staring at the water for a while. The Matriarch canted her head as if listening and whined.

"I didn't mean to do anything wrong," Pio murmured.

"Wrong?" Hamza snapped out of his reverie. "Wrong!" He chuckled and held out his hand. "Let me look at your flute."

Pio clutched the instrument to his chest.

"Don't fret, boy. I'll not break it. I just need a look." He took the flute gently from Pio, turning it over in his hands examining it. "Your pa made this?"

"Yes."

"I need to see those crystals, if you please."

Pio fished the crumpled cloth out of his pocket and unwrapped it. Reverently, he ran his fingers over the dark fragments of crystal before tipping them into Hamza's hand. The moment they touched Hamza's skin, they flared brightly. Pio gasped as the crystals softly pulsed a myriad of colours. The hair on the back of his arms rose and a chill ran down his spine. The Matriarch stared at the crystals and her hackles rose.

Pio's heart raced. He stepped back with a wary glance at her.

Hamza rested his free hand on the Matriarch's head. "All will be well, old mother."

When Pio looked back at him, the crystals lay inert in Hamza's hand. "How? What?"

Hamza smiled at him. "Here you go. Take them back and keep them safe until we reach home." Hamza rose and stretched. "Come on, lad. We've a ways to go and a lot of work to do when we get there."

"Work?"

"Yes. Your pa's made a fine little flute, treasure it. It's made with love and there's a power in that, but you're going to need something special."

Pio felt like he'd missed half of this conversation. "Special?"

"Yep. Pio, when you get to be as old as me and have seen so many winters with bugger all to do, you become a dab hand at woodwork and such, and I can make you a flute to last all your long years—may the goddess grant 'em to you. I want you to have it before the kenati decide they've got the perfect one." He rolled his eyes. "They mean well..."

Pio stared at him, agog, mind whirling with a million questions. *How old is he? How did he know about Isa? Doesn't he like the kenati? Am I talking to Hamza or—*

"Close your mouth, boy," Hamza chuckled. "You get one question, that's it." Rainbow-fire eyes twinkled at Pio.

Hamza waited.

Pio frowned, stepped back, looked Hamza up and down. He touched the man's hand, and a frisson ran down his arm. "Who are you?"

"Hamza," said a multi-timbred voice. "And not," said a feminine voice. "Sometimes the goddess is in me, like now."

A wave of amusement and approval washed over Pio. "Rana?"

"No. I'm much older than her and, between us, she's not really a goddess."

"But—"

"One question, Pio," Hamza said, his usual gruff voice.

"You're... you're going to make me another flute."

"Yes, I'm going to make you a new flute and put those crystals inside it. And a harp too. Do you know how to play a harp?" Pio shook his head. "Never mind you'll learn. Look how well you're doing with the flute. You've got music in your bones, boy." Hamza rubbed his hands together. "Exciting times! You'll be a bard-kenati no-one will forget. Come on." Hamza headed back to camp, his mule and the Matriarch walking sedately by his side.

Pio nodded, slowly following, desperately trying to process what was happening. Questions tumbled in his mind, slippery as eels, vanishing before he could utter them.

Kiriz looked up as they entered the clearing. "You were gone ages!"

Hamza sat and leaned against a tree, pulled his hat down over his face. "I need a bit of a kip. Finding you little rebels takes it out of an old man."

"What were you doing all this time?" Kiriz said.

"Um... The mule needed a big drink." Pio scratched his head, opened his mouth and closed it. He remembered leaving with Hamza and returning. Everything else was blank except—

"Hamza's going to make me a harp."

ABOUT THE AUTHOR

TRACY M JOYCE IS an Australian author of speculative fiction. Tracy has long been a fan of the fantasy genre, but particularly likes novels that deal with deep characterisations and that don't flinch from the gritty realities of life. This and her fascination with the notions of 'moral greyness', that 'good people can do bad things' and that we cannot escape our past provide the inspiration for her writing. Combine that with her love of history, horses and archery and you have Altaica.

She grew up on a farm in rural Victoria, in a picturesque dot on the map known as Glenburn. She spent half of her childhood riding horses and the other half trying to stay out of trouble—the only way she did that was by reading books and writing stories. She now lives in Melbourne with her husband, two cats and two (very) lazy greyhounds.

Tracy holds a BA (Hons) from Monash University, spent many years in a variety of administrative roles and fortunately never gave up on her childhood dream to become a writer. In her spare time she tutors a select and unlucky group of students in English.

Tracy loves to hear from her readers.

www.tracymjoyce.com

PRAISE FOR THE SERIES

"Dang it's good...This is one of those times. This is a series that will keep you wanting more." Jelilat, Goodreads

"Altaica left me speechless. It is a brilliant YA epic fantasy, definitely among the best I've read." Victoria, Goodreads

"Badass from start to finish." Jenna, Goodreads.

"What can I say about Asena Blessed? Altaica (the first book in the series) was a great read, but Asena Blessed is a triumph." Brendan, Goodreads

"After reading Asena Blessed, I realize that Altaica is just a tease, the tip of the iceberg... I read it in one sitting and I felt like I lost a friend once I finished Asena." Arec, Goodreads

A SPECIAL SHORT STORY FOR THOSE OF YOU WHO LOVE THE ASENA!

Still in the planning stages, I hope this will be released in by the end of 2023 or early 2024.

Set toward the end of the Asena wars centuries before Altaica when the clans were new and horse clan struggled to survive in the high plateau.

Find out how the Asena became revered.